Exeunt

BY PETER ABBOT

NOVELS AND NOVELLAS
Librarian
Gukurahundi: Voice of the Lord
Hamiltonians
Quintet: A Novel of COVID-19
Armistice: A Love Story
Plague Year
Duty
Masterson Murders
Exeunt

SHORT STORIES
Gaiety

Exeunt

Peter Abbot

Rock's Mills Press
Rock's Mills, Ontario • Oakville, Ontario
2023

Published by
Rock's Mills Press
www.rocksmillspress.com

This is a work of fiction. Any resemblance to actual places, events, or persons, living or dead, is entirely coincidental.

... the total emptiness for ever,
The sure extinction that we travel to
And shall be lost in always ...
—Philip Larkin (1922–1985), "Aubade"

... let me go, my dearest. Let me go.
We shall not meet again in this life,
So kiss me goodbye now ...
—Raymond Carver (1938–1988), "No Need"

We are and are not.
—Heraclitus, c. 500 BC

1. PAIN

I hate being human.
How long has it taken me to say that – admit that?
So many of us littering this globe as it staggers through the universe.
So many of us born to suffer through painful lives, then die.

Well, I'm not claiming originality; just a final awareness.
And who will read these words anyway?
Who will care, will even notice?
So why bother?

Yes, indeed: why bother? But my excuse is that this morning (Thursday March 18th 2021) I discovered a communication (a Letter, indeed! – in the letter-box, which usually hosts only a bill or two, a charity request or two). And the Letter's envelope had been neatly – no, *beautifully* – addressed; a pen flowing blue ink had been wielded in a firm but elderly hand. "Elderly"? Well, the loopy handwriting had a definitely archaic look.

Pip agreed with that opinion when I showed him the unopened envelope as he sat down opposite me for breakfast (we sometimes but not today have what my Mother would call a "real breakfast", egg and sausage, with toast and marmalade – "Everybody needs a real breakfast" was one of her *diktats*, accompanied by frown and gritted teeth. "You can't work on an empty stomach, ask the Queen.")

"Well, aren't you going to open it?" Pip asked lethargically.

"Yes, and I've just realised who it's from. Let's see if I'm right. My

Aunt Iris, who – Yes. Yes, and it's a real old-fashioned letter, *written*, and superbly legible, grammatically impeccable –"

"Well, *read* it, *read* it, but you don't have to read it out loud, it might be embarrassing, sometimes these old biddies –"

"'Old biddies'? She's got all her marbles, don't worry, *and* she's got *manners* – it's a generation thing of course – and a family thing –" I was absent-mindedly scanning the first page. "*Oh!*"

"'Oh' what? This egg is hard-boiled, did you forget about it in the excitement of looking in the letter-box and finding an actual letter in it? Maybe it's been there for a week –"

"Oh, listen, Pip. She's coming. Here. To visit me. The letter's been forwarded by my neighbour Diana in Hamilton. My Aunt's an Anglican nun."

"*Here*? Coming *here*? When? But I haven't shaved yet –"

Well, no, Pip. She arrived a week later, not long before Easter, and I met her at the Airport. She was clearly exhausted by her long journey from South Africa, with a change-over stop somewhere in Europe (Heathrow I'd guess), then across the Atlantic to Toronto – not a journey I would welcome now, even though I'm a good – what, fifteen years younger than her – she must be about eighty-five! (Mum's older sister – and Mum was what, seventy-three when she died, and their little brother Norman would have been around that age now, even older than me!)

I won't say we were looking forward to Aunt Iris's visit. Pip was in fact quite put out – he didn't *say* so, but I know the signs, bloody-well *should* know them by now.

"Oh, it'll be like *Travels with My Aunt*, you told me that was one of your favourite novels, didn't you?" I opined emolliently. "I know she'll be no trouble, old ladies have such good manners and I'll look after her so you won't have to worry at all, and you once told me, I remember, how much you enjoyed being with *your* aunt for that time after your Mother died when you were a boy –"

"If I did, I lied out of both sides of my mouth – she was a dragon, a gorgon, a witch – I tried hard to like her but didn't succeed, and as you know, I remember I told you, we still talk only at Christmas and Easter. She's my only surviving relative or I wouldn't – Oh, I see what you're doing, Mister! – No, you *don't* set me up as Magwitch, I can see you know very well she'll be *Miss Havisham*, and of course I'm Pip, poor little Pip – but I have no Great Expectations for your Aunt, any more than I have ever had for her extremely troublesome Nephew."

And he stomped off, leaving me to do the washing-up, despite its being a Wednesday. But fortunately I know he's got a heart of gold and – Well, *I* have a heart of gold too, actually – And he also got the wrong novel, maybe he wasn't listening when I demonstrated erudition with my Graham Greene reference. Of course I'm a retired High-school English Teacher (and now volunteer Assistant School Librarian) in my early-seventies – and he's a non-retired Professor of Gerontology fifteen years younger, who still does some teaching and (he implies) research for a book, don't ask me what about (Death?).

We have mostly managed, so far, to steer clear of potentially awkward topics, and instead talk about the endless excitements of the weather, its changeability, its unpredictability. And watch CBC Television. And listen to CBC Radio. And alternate our dwelling-places (my house in Hamilton, or his Toronto condo). And we read and discuss British Great War Poetry (an intense mutual interest). And go on country walks – especially on the Bruce Trail or in the Dundas Valley – to try to stay, in my case, minimally fit. And we try to avoid arguments – since, we have agreed, they exhaust us.

So there I was, at Toronto Airport, with a discreet but artistic sign reading "Sister Martha" (which, she had reminded me in her letter, was her 'official' name as a nun). And the doors opened, the crowd surged noisily forward – But no Sister Martha, until I was about to give up, but then there she was, waving regally. And masked, as we all were, of course (COVID-19 has changed our daily lives in so many ways).

She mostly slept through the first two days. Just as well – we had a major storm, thunder and lightning, the roads and sidewalks were *killers* and I'm sure the hospitals must have been full of broken ancient bones by the time she was ready for the local sights. Except there weren't any sights: everything, even the view from the condo balcony, was still cowering under an endless glittering downpour.

Walking to the bus-stop (both Pip and I travel to further-downtown Toronto by bus) was a slow, ultra-careful parade for Aunt Iris and me. She held my arm. And we met up with Pip before he had become too annoyed to talk; and we had lunch as arranged in Leo's; and I discovered why I hadn't inherited any subtlety and reticence.

Having glanced at the menu, after Mario had led us to the usual discreet corner table, my Aunt glanced casually at Pip and asked, quite loudly, "Are you two homosexual? Do you have sex together?"

I swear Pip actually shuddered.

So I, wondering why she hadn't asked *me* that, before or even while we tottered wetly along College Street holding each other up – or before we set forth together from the condo – so I said, firmly, "You'll be surprised, Aunt Iris, to know that the answer to your query is in the negative. We're both survivors of failed marriages. Pip, whose actual name is Philip, as you might have guessed, has two fine teenage sons at high-school, and we both of us had aggressively high-earning wives, ex-wives, who threw us out to reduce clutter –" And I winked at Pip. Who frowned.

And Aunt Iris, a.k.a. Sister Martha, carefully sipping her cup of black tea, smiled gently. "I always like to know where I am" she murmured.

"Well, you're *not* in your distant nunnery now, and you obviously feel no longer constrained by vows of celibacy or even of politeness and discretion."

Pip could be icily rude. I'd been wondering if he was ill, though he had dismissed my concerned recent enquiries with a frown. But I had known immediately, on my Aunt's arrival, that the disruption of our domestic routine, now combined with what he clearly interpreted as ingratitude and hostility, would destroy any hope of his politely accepting her. Also, like me, he was now suffering from a lack of sleep, since the past two nights had been penetrated unexpectedly by my Aunt's groans and snores (I had not known that ladies snored – my mother said they didn't, *couldn't*; that snoring was just another regrettably uncouth male attribute).

I cleared my throat, opened my mouth –

And Aunt Iris said in her softly resonant way, as she turned towards Pip, "Please do not be upset, my dear. It's merely my inexperience. I have been sequestered from the wider society for so long that my manners *are* indeed somewhat rusty. I don't *intend* to be rude. Whereas *you* have the luxury of sophistication, experience, sociability, generosity, discretion and self-control."

Pip was silenced. He cleared his throat and paid attention to his soup. Later, as Pip and I drank our coffee, Aunt Iris delicately sipped her Lady Grey tea ("definitely superior to *Earl* Grey, I introduced *both* of them to the other Sisters") and commented on the restaurant's decor, slow service, and chattering clientele.

Do I give a severe portrait of my Aunt? Yes. But I think, I hope, it also conveys an affectionate disappointment that her visit was so short. *More* than short (or should that be *less* than short; no) – She left us after four days – with fervent gratitude for my "meeting her at the Airport and putting up with her", while "tolerating her need to catch up on sleep, and not resenting her rusty social behaviour". (Was that a dig, or merely a hostile ambiguity?) "But tomorrow will be Maundy Thursday. And I must be at our Mother House for Easter. They will collect me and drive me there."

In the end, I liked and even admired her. Quite a dame, I thought – with even some pride. Pip never did like her (she and her visit were topics to be avoided, after her departure!). He wasn't willing, I think, to recognise what my Mother might, in a kind moment, have called her sister-in-law's "sterling qualities". (And indeed my Aunt *did* remind me of my Mother and *her* sterling qualities, her sharp scrutiny of distressingly slack male behaviour.)

What Pip missed were, first, the story of her unremitting fight to save her Nunnery and its long-established Teacher-Training College, in the Eastern Cape of South Africa. I'll try to summarise her account of that (given to me the evening after that memorable restaurant lunch in Toronto – Pip was out at a Meeting, as he sometimes was, and my Aunt and I had post-prandially imbibed the contents of a bottle of South African wine that she had purchased as a gift for me at Cape Town Airport).

We were sitting comfortably in the two arm-chairs; the electric-fire had warmed the room to an almost-soporific degree; and I had made us a *boboetie* and *melk-tart* that she had praised and relished.

When she suddenly said "Thank you, my dear Nephew, for another enjoyable, memorable day. I'll be leaving you tomorrow morning, as you know, and quite soon I'll be dead."

Silence. While I wondered if she had intended to say what she had just said – was she 'tiddly' (my Father's word), did she actually *mean* what she'd just said?

She looked into my eyes. "Yes, I do mean that, my dear Nephew. It's been arranged for a while. My Doctor in South Africa has worked it all out with a colleague of his here in Ontario, and with the Community – you wouldn't have known of course, but the Mother House of our now-defunct Nunnery is here in Ontario, that's how I became a Sister, and of course they have known all the details for almost a year – you see, I have a rare cancer that is eating away, *has* eaten away, *is* eating away – No, we won't get into details, I'm not in very great pain, I take pills – And I told them over here that you would be meeting me and that I wanted to spend some of my final time here on earth with *you* – and then my final Easter with my Canadian Sisters. But when I received no reply to the letter I wrote you from South Africa, I wondered if – but I knew I could always telephone our Mother House from the Airport if you had not appeared – so of course I decided to come just as planned – And there you were! In answer to my prayer. God has been so good to me." She suddenly leaned forward and I saw that her hands were trembling. "And that's – and now you know –"

"Yes. Thank you for telling me, please don't upset yourself, Aunt Iris."

"But I must also summarise, as I said I would, the final state of the Nunnery that I tried, *we* really did try, so hard, with God's help, to save – but God has a different and better plan, I know – it's in His hands, and if the Nunnery can't be saved by human-beings – well, we know by now that it can't be, we worked and worked and prayed and prayed, but in the end it just couldn't be saved – the new Government Minister said so, very clearly – there's Politics at work, of course, but also the buildings *are* old, in fact decrepit, alas – like me, like all four of us, we four surviving Sisters, I mean – the other three have also found a good place to die. And so that's how my story ends. God sends Death to us all. Even to Nuns and a Nunnery serving Him."

My Aunt sighed deeply. It was hard to know what to say, find any warm words of respect and comfort. But I tried. I even asked if she would like me to be with her when she died.

"No. God will be with me, and Jesus and Mary and the Angels. And the Doctor and a Nurse. You'd only clutter up the room. We'll say our farewell here, my dear Nephew."

Next morning a taxi, ordered earlier by me at my Aunt's request, arrived soon after we had eaten breakfast and I had taken her suitcase down to the main door. Pip had already left for 'work' (mainly research in the Toronto University Library for the putative book whose gestation he had recently revealed to me), bidding her an airy farewell.

"I wish I had more suitable clothes" she said. "But this coat covers all, thank goodness. Beggars can't be choosers is what my Mother – your paternal Grandmother – used to say."

I looked hard at her, trying to force her appearance into my memory. Longish grey hair, sunburnt deeply-lined face, alert grey eyes, bad teeth, thin-lipped mouth, jutting cheeks, scrawny neck – all above a boy-slim body swathed in a shabby drooping pale-blue dress under a ratty old brown coat. I imagined her standing in front of a blackboard within a big thatched hut, teaching small smiling African kids how to add and subtract and to recite the Lord's Prayer. Though not in that coat surely. And of course she had also been teaching Black and White and Coloured *women* how to teach children effectively.

We heard the taxi arrive. "Come here, Nephew" she said. "Let me kiss you goodbye. And please say Farewell for me to your funny friend. I'll see you next in Paradise – so long as you behave yourself and keep well away from drugs and liquor, and cynicism and irreligion. No, there's no need to carry that, I can manage" as she picked up her suitcase, after kissing me lightly on my forehead and putting on her mask. "And live a good life. Always. Worship God your Father and Jesus His Son. And be loving. And grateful for all our blessings. Be kind. Be honest. Be generous. And loving."

She was holding one of my hands and looking deeply into my eyes. I kissed a leathery cheek, then pulled away from her, opened the front-door, and waved to the taxi-driver.

Then she was gone.

And, to my surprise, a hole opened up in my life.

So we join the long procession.
Where are we going?
We do not know, we cannot know.
Life gets us ready for death.
That's all it is?

So move on, move on, move on, move on.
Move on.
Move.
On.

2. GONE

Late May 2021. A shock. A shock to Canada.

Two hundred and fifteen buried corpses of children have just been discovered (using a 'novel x-ray technique', apparently) 'in unmarked graves' near the old Kamloops Residential School which had been administered by the Roman Catholic Church in British Columbia, under the aegis of the Canadian Government.

No children – no children – should die like that, isolated from their parents and families. And in physical and psychological pain.

The shock of this new information has been nationwide, reminding all Canadians, and informing people around the world, of the abuse and suffering, and the many deaths, of First Nations (Native Indian) children – deaths that occurred within Residential Schools in various Canadian Provinces.

Children were taken from parents and families, to be educated by missionary-teachers employed by Christian denominations, under the policy and mandate of the Canadian Government – from the time of the first Prime Minister, Sir John A. Macdonald, until, it seems, quite recently.

Destructive effects of that policy have been known for many years, knowledge endorsed by testimony from those who as children had endured the sudden and absolute separation from their family, belief-system, language and society; so as to be 'educated in accordance with Western Christian values' – precipitating grievous personal and social consequences.

Not only is this remembered and resented within the afflicted communities for its painful, destructive effects, but it has also been publicised widely within Canadian society, in recent years, through the testimony of survivors and their families, and also through the efforts of prominent and admired activists and artists, like the singer Gord Downey.

Yet today's news has shocked Canadians, and has reverberated in other countries – at a time when, during the continuing COVID trail of illness, death and confusion, we are, often with angry impatience and repudiation, trapped in a state of confused uncertainty and even, sometimes, panic.

So how should the Canadian Government act now? And what should, or *can*, each of us do? What is our responsibility, our duty?

Two hundred and fifteen corpses of children. 215. Which signify also the wider destruction that we mindlessly cause, all too often: the suffering and death of fellow humans and fellow creatures; the ongoing devastation of the natural world we all inhabit.

Sin. *Our* sin. Death. *Their* death, and ultimately *our spiritual death.* And our actual physical death, as a species, in time.

How many children suffered and died altogether in those Residential Schools? And what remedy, what atonement, what contrition, is possible – especially when so few of us are likely to accept any responsibility at all?

Yes, pull down statues of Sir John A. Macdonald: he was responsible for the original ruinous Policy, wasn't he? Yes, the Churches that executed the Policy, that ran the Residential Schools on behalf of the Canadian Government: they must all accept their responsibility, must Apologise and financially compensate Survivors of the Residential School system. The Pope must apologise! And yes, the Government itself carries responsibility – the original, basic responsibility; and must atone, must make all possible reparation.

And when those actions have been performed (if they ever are – if they ever are), what then? Will atonement be complete? Can righteousness be restored?

In a complex chaotic federal governance system, with many

often-conflicting responsibilities, and a large number of jostling authorities spread across this huge land, how will adequate change and remediation happen? How – and when? Can it happen even while COVID and its death-count grows and grows? (What is that count now in Canada? I've just checked. Nearly four million deaths! Can that be right?)

– And a CBC news-report, just this morning (Thursday 24th June 2012): another large number of unmarked graves (hundreds) have been discovered near another Residential School (this time in Saskatchewan, I think). Oh, oh. The horror and the sorrow and the shame continue to expand and deepen.

My Aunt Iris (who returned to Canada recently, after living most of her life abroad, as an Anglican nun) told me that, when she was deeply troubled about human suffering and evil, and had prayed for three hours, begging God to alleviate human suffering (especially the suffering of children whom she had taught and known well, in *apartheid* South Africa), she would listen to her Religious Order's CD of Mahler's song-cycle *Kindertotenlieder (Songs on the Death of Children)* ("sung gloriously, unforgettably, by Dietrich Fischer-Dieskau"), as a partial antidote for her distress ("and to assure me again, and the Devil, that he can never, never, never win. *Amor vincit omnia.*"). And, she told me, that action had made it possible for her to sleep through the night.

I have that CD. She was given it when the South African branch of her Order was forced to close, she told me. And she left that CD on the bed where she had slept during her recent short visit – left it deliberately, I believe, as a gift of love and consolation. (I had told her, when we chatted during our final breakfast together, that she reminded me greatly of my Mother – and, embarrassingly, I had actually become tearful while telling her that).

So now I will dig out the CD. I think I need to listen to it again now. Especially as the news about those often-long-past deaths of Canadian First Nations children has also set me to recalling the death of not only my Aunt, but also, more recently, of my friend Philip (Pip, as I always called him – as he *instructed* me to call him).

Pip. Oh, Pip. Gone too. Gone. And he too, like my Aunt, left me something precious.

But his death was such a shock – a sudden and very severe heart-attack, one of the doctors told me, and it seemed to silence him almost completely. Or was the cause actually COVID, as I suspected later? – Or both? He was so breathless when I got to him after the University Librarian called me. But his death was so sudden, so quick – though Ive been told he had been one of the liveliest, most vigorous, men you could ever hope to know. And yet he was just – just gone. Gone. And he was some fifteen years younger than me.

I first met him, saw him, was it just last summer? On the board-walk in the Nature Reserve near Petrel Point, on the Bruce Peninsula. During this Plague, of course. This COVID-19.

A sharp sunny day and I was taking a break on one of the board-walk's benches-with-a-view, when a dog came galloping round the corner, dragging behind her a puffing middle-aged man. Who sat down heavily on the other end of my bench, and gasped after a moment "I hope you don't mind – I'll keep a good COVID distance from you – so don't worry – and I've got a mask in my pocket if –"

"Oh please don't bother – they all say, the medical experts, don't they, that there's little or no danger of catching it in the open air. If you keep your distance."

The dog, a plump panting pug, threw itself heavily against my legs and gazed snufflingly up at me out of bulging saucer-eyes.

"Just cuff her if she's a nuisance, and push her away, she won't bite. She's called Dolly, after, you know, Dolly Parton – who, I hasten to say, doesn't ever snuffle like that, as far as I know. She belongs to a friend. Who *does* snuffle like that, now that I think of it. My name's Pip. And you are –?"

"Pip – You said Pip?"

"Philip Ian Patrick – but I disliked all those names, so – Pip."

"Oh. Derrick, I'm Derrick." And after a short pause, during which I patted Dolly's broad head, "Do you live up here?"

"No, just got away from the City for the weekend. With two friends. Who don't walk their dog enough. How about you?"

"Oh, I have a Cottage just along the road, towards Red Bay. Actually it's an old family place falling into ruin, but good enough for a short stay. You probably passed it walking here."

"Must have. My friends' Cottage is *in* Red Bay. Married? Children?"

"Look, if we're going to have a deep, revealing, getting-to-know-you conversation, why don't we have it over a beer outside my Cottage? I'm thirsty. And I can offer cheese and olives in lieu of lunch." A more decisive response than usual, but I was clearly the elder, and feeling a bit irritated, no doubt, by the abrupt intrusion into my morning walk.

Pip laughed. "All right. Thanks. Your risk, but I guess we're both probably safe enough. Until we get Vaccinated or the next Variant comes along."

So that's how our friendship began.

Neither of us was gay. Both of us were discarded husbands. And Pip, at fifty-five, some fifteen years younger than me, was the father of two sons, in their late teens – one of whom, he told me, was impatiently hoping to start University this Fall, COVID permitting. Like so many of his peers.

We sat outside, in the sunlight, Pip and I, at the decrepit picnic-table – oh, the shame of it, if noticed by the neighbours! My wife, ex-wife, would have said that; no doubt *did* say exactly that. And now we two discarded husbands sat there, each with a can of Rickard's Red, the only Canadian beer I know at all well. And Dolly lying flat-out and uncomplainingly at Pip's feet, snuffling in her dreams.

Strange that only then did I feel shy and tense. You see, I've never been at ease in social situations. Ask my wife Stella. Ex-wife. That was always one of her complaints about me – though she also objected when I "tried to make friends with her work-partners" in her posh law-firm – especially with the one of them who, like me, loved classical music and opera. And was reputed to be gay.

But we didn't say much, on that first occasion, Pip and I, about our ex-marital situations.

I told him, briefly, hesitantly, unexpectedly, that I'd never felt I measured up to Stella's expectations – which were, I thought – but didn't say, then – based on memories of three aggressive brothers and a hectoring father. (Or that was my rationalisation.) Her mother liked me, I think, but she died couple of years after Stella and I got married. No children – and I was blamed for that, fairly or unfairly, but she refused to consider adoption. So our shallow-rooted marriage slowly withered on its vine, and in the end I think both of us were relieved, even happy, to bury it. And then, years later, she –

"Sorry, that was probably more than you needed or wanted to know. And I don't usually talk about my personal feelings like that, especially at a first meeting. Sorry!"

"Don't be." Pip was brief, and perceptive. (Always, or almost always, I discovered later.) "*My* wife died – quite recently, when our kids were young teenagers. Now *they* look after *me* and worry about my health. And get angry at COVID for wrecking their lives. Poor guys – I told them there's lots more suffering to come! – No, no, I didn't – don't look so shocked, that would have been stupidly cruel of course! I'm not such a jerk. I was just joking!"

Why am I writing all that, now, about my first meeting with Pip? When I intended to write more about the 215 dead Residential School children? If I had any more to say. Do I?

Well, those deaths – the deaths of helpless children ripped away from their families – must have got me thinking about Pip's death – which was not so long ago. The pain and sorrow of that, too – I still feel it so deeply – unassuaged, unassuageable. I sometimes feel desolate. Truly desolate. Suicidal. If the loss of the 215 was as traumatic, and it very surely was, at least in most cases – if it was as traumatic for their mothers and fathers and families – Children just discarded anonymously into remote graves! But maybe I haven't got all the facts right. Does one ever? Some of the teachers of those children must surely have been good people trying to do a good job?

And – Well, I guess it was that connection – Death, which comes to us all, but, in the case of those children, resulted in a virtual silence that endured for so many years, a painful national as well as personal silence – which maybe, God willing, has now been broken fully and for ever –

And is there anything else for me to say now?

No. Human beings, and, who knows, animals, birds, insects, plants, all delivered from the huge unending black Void into Life and Suffering – but hopefully also, if they're fortunate – and we know some, many, are not – delivered healthy and happy into Love and Joy – and only then, finally, into Death – which we think of as darkness and endless alienation, don't we? – but, who knows, may be something quite other – something gloriously beyond any human comprehension – But now I'm rambling – all too obviously –

As Pip always said – Even just hours before his death, he said it, that it was all a mystery: Life, Death. It was something obvious that he'd said before, when, as far as I know, he had no inkling of his own approaching premature death, of death at all – Yet, he had told me once, as a boy he had been in a serious accident, and death was clearly something that really troubled him – and if I tried to move the conversation away from that subject, he would get annoyed, "You just try to evade any serious thinking about any serious topic, don't you? You're so pathetic. *Pathetic!* Why do I even try to have a serious conversation with you at all?"

Yes, Pip, you were right, I'm essentially a light-weight, that's what my Ex-wife said, more than once. Or expressed silently, pursed lips and half-smile. No ambition, Derrick, no ambition! And of course *she* was right too. But, also of course, it's much, much too late for me to change now. If it was ever possible. For better, for worse – I'm

"Just as I am." Just Derrick – I hate that name, always *have* hated it.

And now I'll listen to Mahler's *Songs on the Death of Children*, and then I'll think of my Aunt Iris, and my Parents, and Pip, and even Stella, and of the 215 dead children, and try to visualize them, and pray for them, and for us all. They're all dead, and I'll be dead soon. We'll *all* be dead soon. Dead and gone.

Pip once said something like this to me: "We can't comprehend the huge population of China right now – and just think, just try to imagine, the billions, trillions, the countless mass of human-beings who have already passed through their lives into death – in all the centuries, all the millennia, of the Earth's existence. In all the countries of the world.

"I have just been reading a book that one of my colleagues insisted on lending me – here, listen to this: 'What more than anything else appears to torment men of my age … is the nearness of death … But what a poor dotard must he be who has not learnt in the course of a long life that death is not a thing to be feared?' And who said that? Sure makes me feel like *I'm* one of those dotards.

"And who said *this*? 'Dying is nothing to fear. It is the most wonderful experience of your life.' Oh, you *don't know*? Haven't I already quoted that?

No, just thought it, Pip – and without conviction, too, I guess.

He wasn't finished. "First quotation is a translation from an 'Essay on Old Age' by Cicero, who lived during the century before the birth of Christ. Second is by Elisabeth Kubler-Ross, our respected American near-contemporary – but I should have added that she ends 'It all depends on how you have lived your life.' Which – well, it somewhat muddies the water?

"Did you know, did I ever tell you, that I'm an inveterate collector of quotations? Most of which do not stick in my pea-brain. Lots more about Death, but I won't throw them at you now when you're so busy doing bloody nothing as usual, and thinking about nothing too, probably– lazy sod! Maybe later. So get on with your empty life. And I *did* find the file of my collected quotations the other day. Which I'll toss as soon as I've glanced through it." (But he didn't.)

That was perhaps the longest speech Pip ever directed at me. Remembered by me with, I hope, some accuracy. But of course he *was* a Professor and a Gerontologist, and taught Undergraduates who might later work in Seniors' Homes: that of course explained the collection of quotations, which I've inherited, along with a mass of mind-improving books on such esoteric topics as How to Grow Old and Still Smile that I must now find means and energy to dispose of.

The aftermath of even a single death can be overwhelming for a survivor. *I* have certainly come near to collapse. Depression! Even decisions that should be simple, like disposing of clothes, can become causes of renewed grief. And I had *two* aftermath-of-death situations to manage, quite close together, Pip's wasn't the first – though I should also recall that somehow the double desolation seemed to lighten the emotional load; maybe one's emotions cope better with excess since that can actually blunt the sharpness of loss, distract one ("Distraction from distraction by distraction", T.S.Eliot), even enable one to forget one's loss temporarily – and now I'm recalling how, in a war situation, the first deaths are so intense, and then the impact of later losses diminishes progressively – for, as Eliot put it, "Humankind cannot bear much reality."

Stella's death was a sudden devastating shock – yes, I've been trying to forget it, evade it – still, now. I never spoke of it to Pip, even when he asked me to. It was the result of an accident, one of those sudden pile-ups – when she was driving home along the QEW Highway in a snowstorm. After the day's work in her legal office in Toronto. How many years ago? Eight? Ten?

I felt almost a stranger at her Funeral. Which was of course before COVID struck, so there was a Mass in her Church, attended by friends and family (her sister and brother, the four nieces and nephews), and a procession in our vehicles to her interment in the City Cemetery. Nobody spoke to me afterwards, or at any point – except the Priest, briefly – and probably most of them wouldn't have known or remembered by then that she'd even been married.

Her brother telephoned me after the burial to ask if there was anything I would like from among her possessions; I said No, and thanked him for asking. (I have too many possessions – what will become of them when I "kick the bucket"? – my Father's elegant expression, that! Oh, Dad, yes, I remember *your* funeral too: one of the several unremarkably studding my life – most lives probably; and yes, I remember my Mother sobbing and sobbing as I hugged her. But I wasn't able to be at *her* funeral – why? Was I sick? Can't recall. Maybe I *was* there and just can't bear to remember.)

But Pip. He insisted that there should be no funeral, no notice of his death in the local newspaper. "But why?" I asked. "And why are we talking about that now?"

"No business of yours, Mister D. *You* can make *your* decision, *I've* made *mine*. So just accept it. I saw my Doctor today" and he smiled.

"Oh?" was what I think I said, stupidly, but somehow I did know what was coming, didn't I? Must have done. For I had seen him wincing, gasping; I had offered again to drive him to his Doctor's office, but No, didn't I think he was capable of driving that short distance? He was just fine! – And, next Spring, he said, he intended to drive us to the Cottage at Red Bay – which he said he was looking forward to doing, just as soon as the weather allowed.

But of course he died before that, about a year ago actually. A sudden heart-attack. Have I already said this? And he had arranged, some time previously, for his body to be quietly cremated – with just his sons and me present. It reminded me – maybe he meant it to – of the end of that Truffaut film with Jeanne Moreau that we found we had both loved and admired in the distant past, long before we met: *Jules et Jim*. "You Jules, me Jim" he once said. Yes, yes, Pip, I guess our relationship *was* a bit like that. Without sex, and without a Catherine between us, to roil our relationship – brief as it was.

And so here I am. Stumbling on, alone. Towards my own end.

3. WORD

When we partnered, Pip and I lived, alternately, in his Toronto condo and my Hamilton house – not a convenient arrangement, merely a temporary one, we said, pending a decision to sell one of them. But which one? He disliked his Toronto condo: "I always preferred a house, with a garden, that's what we had when I was growing up". I wish he'd been given more time to retire and enjoy living with me, in this house – (It was cruel, God-if-there-is-a God, to take him so soon – depriving me of his company, so soon, so very soon!)

But we did have enough time for some good conversations. Good memorable conversations. And arguments!

Pip, in public, was usually terse. Partly, I thought, this was a compensatory effect of his career as a Professor of Gerontology. One of his ex-students, recognising me from a long-ago high-school History class – in the local supermarket, just yesterday, both of us waiting in the queue and both masked of course – She said when I mentioned Pip (I find I want to talk about him all the time! – she hadn't heard about his death), "What a wonderful Prof he was, we were so lucky to have him – so humane, and his lectures were so good – he was so popular, students always rushed to enrol in his classes." Pip would have scoffed, if I'd been able to report that conversation, but I totally believed the student.

Yes, Pip. There was also just time for him to instil into my pea-brain some of his unexpected love for British Great War Poetry: "I always insist on calling it that, *Great War Poetry* not *First World War Poetry* – the *Great* applying to the Poetry, not to the War, which, as we all know, was totally *ghastly*. 'The poetry is in the pity' is what Wilfred Owen wrote. And 'What passing-bells for *those who die as cattle*?' He was courageous, and honest, Owen. Those Poets were true heroes – some of them in combat, *all* of them as writers, truth-tellers – they insisted on writing the *truth* of what they saw and what they experienced. They did humanity proud, and if war could ever be acceptable, morally acceptable, they made it so."

Resisting that final comment, which puzzled me (can war ever be made acceptable?), I still thought admiringly "That's what you said in your Gerontology lectures? And when you started lecturing, maybe some of your students were ex-soldiers or ex-Peace Officers who had been surrounded by the Dead and could have actually seen and experienced something of the poets' truth-telling. The truth about the painful deaths of soldiers, like those in the Trenches of the First World War. So many deaths, so many deaths in so many ways. In so many wars."

And, like so many of those poets, Pip has died quite young – he must have been in his fifties? Or sixties? – yes, my memory is deteriorating fast, but I think that's right. So *not* so young, in years, actually, but still *too young to die*. I miss him more, I think, every day – more than I could ever have expected.

Yes, but we differed about our most-admired War-poets and most-admired War-poems. Owen was *the* Great War Poet for Pip: no argument or qualification tolerated. Though he admired other War-poets and War-poems. However, after reading twice through the Penguin *First World War Poetry*, which extended my knowledge and revived my love of those poems (he gave me a copy inscribed "To a dullard, *q.v.* p. 191"), *my* choice was and always will be Isaac Rosenberg, who faced Death full-on; that's what I told Pip, and quoted from the two Rosenberg poems that had impressed me so very greatly: "Returning, We Hear the Larks" ("Death could drop from the dark / As easily as song...") and, above all, "Dead Man's Dump" ("The air is loud with death... They left this dead with the older dead... Here is one not long dead… And our wheels grazed his dead face.") Yes, Rosenberg faced Death full-on, unflinchingly, eternally, absolutely.

But before I met Pip – long before, when I was a child maybe two years old, then again when I was seven or eight years old, or a bit older, I was influenced by my two uncles. Before and after they went to war. One was my Mother's younger brother; the other was my Father's younger brother. "They were such very good friends, from the moment they met" my Mother once said.

I still have, somewhere, a couple of small black-and-white photos, taken by my Mother with her little primitive Brownie camera, photos of myself as a very small boy, in 1940 or so: in one, being held by her brother Eddie, in our Toronto garden; in the other, being held by my Father's brother Norman, on the station-platform, with the troop-train behind him. Both young men in uniform of course, smiling determinedly, bravely; on their way to save the British Empire and all Humanity from Hitler and his Nazi hordes. As I recall those two small photos, and my small abashed self, and the two Uncles – who both survived, both Came Home –

And now here he is: ugly bald Old Man, barely-recognisable snorty Norman, sitting opposite me in my Hamilton home, eyes closed tight! Years and years ago.

But when I had mentioned the War, and his involvement in it, cautiously, after his explosively angry responses to my earlier gambits, Uncle Norman had muttered, after a short silence – muttered what?

I tried again. Which elicited an angry "Fuck you, get off my fuckin' back, will you." But that was followed by his eyes slowly opening, focussing, and an abrupt throat-clearing. Then a growl of "Look here, my boy" (which was, I suddenly recalled, how my Father had tended to address me – when he did address me). "I'm old, an old man now, gotta give me some respect, hey – keep your distance, hey. So you're my Nephew, that's what he told you, right? *Right?* But they always lie, everybody lies, so gotta take my time. Need more sleep, right, right? Then maybe we'll talk."

And we actually did.

When I was looking through Pip's Papers, to dispose of files containing old lecture-notes, I came across one labelled DEATH Qs, and found that it was a collection of quotations about Death that he may have incorporated in some of his lectures.

So I'm going to copy out some of them here, representative ones that I found *I* respond to. Some of them are copied from the *Hamilton Spectator* (my local newspaper), like this first one – but of course Pip's transcriptions may not be strictly accurate always, and his scrawl isn't always easy to decipher:

The way most people feel about death: We know it exists, but we do not want to acknowledge it and we do not want to linger in its presence.

Yes, true. This next one is from another, different article or review: under Pip's scrawled added title, 'Death illiteracy':

… unless we begin to talk about death, to 'befriend' it, we will see suffering on a massive scale. This is like the perfect storm in North America. There will be too many people with too many needs, and not enough of us able to support them. We won't know what to do with all these dying people…

'Befriending' death! Before the future disaster of over-population or global-warming strikes! And a final excerpt, apparently, taken from another article:

Only about one person in five dies at home. [In North America.] We rarely have a direct experience of death. We see graphic scenes of violence and death in the movies or on TV but these images distance us from death; they have little impact on our daily lives.

Those were more-or-less contemporary comments. They illustrate some divergent and even contradictory opinions representative of our confused responses to death. The following much-older set of opinions, also collected by Pip, illustrate a range of responses to the immitigable (I love that word!) fact of death:

CICERO: … what a poor dotard must he be who has not learnt in the course of a long life that death is not a thing to be feared?

SOPHOCLES: To die is to begin to live.

DMITRI SHOSTAKOVICH: Death is the real end, there will be nothing afterwards, nothing.

SCOTT SYMONS: We are put on this earth to celebrate… Death renders life magnificent.

WINIFRED HOLTBY: Death balances the picture… It makes even cruelty fall into place. It is completion.

GEORGE ORWELL: The major problem of our time is the decay of the belief in personal immortality.

ELISABETH KUBLER-ROSS: Dying is nothing to fear. It is the most wonderful experience of your life.

And, looking again through Pip's well-thumbed copy of the *Penguin Book of First World War Poetry*, I saw that he had marked passages in various poems, among them:

Such, such is Death: no triumph: no defeat:
Only an empty pail, a slate rubbed clean,
A merciful putting-away of what has been.
(Charles Hamilton Sorley, "Two Sonnets")

Cover him, cover him soon!
    And with thick-set
Masses of memoried flowers –
    Hide that red wet
    Thing I must somehow forget.
(Ivor Gurney, "To His Love")

The place was rotten with dead; green clumsy legs
High-booted, sprawled and grovelled along the saps,
And trunks, face downward, in the sucking mud,
Wallowed like trodden sand-bags loosely filled;
And naked sodden buttocks, mats of hair,
Bulged, clotted heads slept in the plastering slime.
(Siegfried Sassoon, "Counter-Attack")

Of them who running on that last high place
Breasted even the rapture of bullets, or went up
On the hot blast and fury of hell's upsurge,
Or plunged and fell away past this world's verge,
Some say God caught them even before they fell.
(Wilfred Owen, "Spring Offensive")

And then there are contemporary and near-contemporary poems, copied out untidily and in probable haste. And of course there was a quotation from the ubiquitous Dylan Thomas poem that I have never liked (why? Too angry?):

Do not go gentle into that good night.
Rage, rage against the dying of the light.

Then a set of elegies. By Thomas Hardy (1840–1928), who, after 'retiring' from novel-writing, wrote poetry in his final years. From the first of Hardy's Elegies (six poems, according to Pip's annotated photocopies), "The Going":

Why did you give no hint that night
That quickly after the morrow's dawn,
And calmly, as if indifferent quite,
You would close your term here, up and be gone
Where I could not follow...

Never to bid goodbye,
Or lip me the softest call,
Or utter a wish for a word, while I
Saw morning harden upon the wall,
Unmoved, unknowing
That your great going
Had place that moment, and altered all...

Well, well! All's past amend,
Unchangeable. It must go.
I seem but a dead man held on end
To sink down soon...

I remember I was actually reading, re-reading, these poems when I heard the post arrive – heard it being deposited noisily in my post-box. Checking later, I found a letter among the invoices and advertisements. It was from the Office of the Mother Superior, The Nunnery, Guelph, Ontario. And here it is:

April 19, 2021
Dear Mr Abbot:

You don't know me, but I know of you from our very dear Sister Martha, who told me that you are her Nephew and provided me with your name and address.

This is to let you know that Sister Martha has passed away into God's loving care, after suffering bravely in the service of Our Lord Jesus Christ for many years.

She requested that I should tell you again how very grateful she was for the kind and generous hospitality you provided as she was returning to our Mother House, after her long, unremitting efforts in South Africa to support and extend Christian education there.

If you should wish to visit her grave, in our little cemetery, you would of course be very welcome.

I trust your Easter was truly joyous.
Yours in Christ,
Mother Winifred
(Order of Christian Martyrs)

It was then I knew, as I had earlier hoped, that my Aunt Iris had been given what used to be called 'the needle of mercy' (now a 'physician-assisted' death). During her brief visit to me, she had sometimes seemed to be in considerable pain, which she attempted to conceal. Since her cancer had, according to the little she revealed to me, developed to a severe, inoperable degree, and seemed to be causing her increasing distress, I was relieved to know that her suffering was over; even though I had very much hoped to see her again. I had been thinking, after she left, of so many questions that I never asked then – and now never to be asked, of course.

I remember hoping and believing, during my hospital-volunteering some years ago, that one day it would be legally possible for such deaths as Aunt Iris's to be administered openly, under legal protection – administered openly to all who are in extreme pain and fervently desire release – And then the hypocrisy of deaths being administered in secrecy and complicity could end. (I never discussed this issue with Pip, but I'm sure he would have agreed.)

And now, in Canada, we do have Physician-assisted death, as a legal option for those who, like my Aunt, are in severe final pain.

My only hesitation is that, while citizens of some countries in the wealthy West can legally choose a medically-supervised death if they are in extreme, irremediable pain, the citizens of many other countries do not have that option – may never have that option. So, openly or surreptitiously, it will continue to be tacitly assumed by us that the suffering and deaths of Third World citizens are of much less or even of *no* significance?

So – Must even Death be subject to prejudice, poverty, international politics? No! No.

(Am I ending this disquisition-on-Death too abruptly? All right, yes. But maybe that's appropriate. What do you think, Pip?)

There are such varied responses, around the world, to death – responses determined by circumstance, religious belief, personal idiosyncrasy. To some extent we are all subject to our inheritance, including its degree of tolerated personal freedom: where we are born, our society's values, our experiences in life, our poverty or wealth, the extent of our ability to control our behaviour. So much, I know, is merely statement of the obvious. But in that variable flux, we learn, early or late, that each of us must come to an end. Must endure that final fact of each life. Must die. So why do we cling to life? But we do. So – "Provide, provide!" If you can.

"We are and are not."

4. LOSS

A sharp knock at the front-door. I opened it cautiously. There had been reports and warnings on the radio and in the local newspaper. "Murders by the Mob", advice to keep doors locked and to avoid strangers.

When was this? Must have been sometime during the mid-1980s? Or early 1990s?

Which was a very painful period in my life – a period that the intrusion of my Aunt Iris, her death and the death of Pip have brought back into my memory. But mostly it was painful because that was when my marriage finally and irrevocably stumbled, crumbled and died.

Of course, in my few conversations with Aunt Iris, I never referred to that period, or to my divorce. And of course Aunt Iris said nothing to me about my divorce – probably *knew* nothing about it, for she was by the 1980s busy saving Africans for Christ. – No, I should take that snide comment back – we hardly knew each other. "Crying heals no wounds" – did my Mother say that?

My Wife had left me and moved to Toronto. We had divorced, (quite amicably – or at least I hadn't contested her account of the marriage, or questioned the verdict) and I had moved into this house where, as she predicted, I am immured. First I rented it, then I bought it.

Even Pip commented mildly (for him) about my apparent withdrawal from life. "That's like being dead while you're still alive, like being a zombie" he said. Oh. Ouch.

But now *he's* dead and I'm still living – or partly living. Aunt Iris perceived, I think, that I'm spiritually and psychologically dead. Maybe she thought an infusion of Mahler and Dietrich Fischer-Dieskau might galvanise me. Dead when I'm still alive! Oh.

Here and now, I am back in my house in Hamilton, cleaning and tidying it; mainly by chucking out old files and their contents, and putting books and small disposable items in cardboard boxes. (Getting ready for death – yes, Pip!) After his (unannounced online) funeral, I reported his death to the rental-company that owns his Toronto apartment, which he had rented since the death of his wife; and was told that all his possessions must be removed by the end of this month, i.e., in a couple days now.

It was a tiring task, I quickly realised – which made me recognise anew the need to get on with the tidying of *my* quarters and the disposal of *my* effects! Pip's two sons had said, vaguely and without enthusiasm, after their Dad's death and cremation, that they'd be "happy to help" but then did not actually *produce* that help, and I was reluctant to bug them, especially when, because of COVID, they are confined by Ontario's Lockdown, and missing the conventional end-of-the-school-year dances and parties and hijinks. So I still need to complete the disposal of his stuff very soon – I know I'm stalling by tidying *my* stuff first – Evasion!

And now I'm recalling Uncle Norman's visit – compulsively, obsessively? But also to try to set myself free of all, or as many as possible, of my ugly memories. All those before I met Pip, who gave me so many good ones. Oh, if only one *could* clear out one's mind! Anyway – back to the past –

I had opened the door of my house, cautiously, to a stranger or was he? He looked a bit familiar.

"Hi" he said.

"Hullo. If you're looking for Dr Plasket, he lives next-door."

"I know him of course – or at least who he is, Professor of Sociology at the University? It was *you* I was looking for – Your neighbour Mrs Miller told me she thought you were home – I guess you didn't hear me knocking earlier?"

"Oh, now I recognise you! Aren't you Brother Martin?"

"Indeed, I am. And you're Derrick, I can't remember your surname, sorry, but we know each other from Good Passage. Volunteering, giving help and advice to ex-prison-inmates just out of jail? They had your address in the Passage office."

"Yes, but I had to stop doing that volunteering, a few years ago. Doctor's orders. Oh, sorry – keeping you standing there. Why don't you come in?"

And only then I noticed, to his left, nearby, another man – an elderly man. Standing very still, leaning against the wall with his eyes closed.

"No – thank you, I shouldn't come in, but I have someone here with me who would very much like –"

"Oh." I was hesitant, puzzled.

Brother Martin went to the old man, put an arm round him and, as the old man opened his eyes, brought him toward me.

"Fuckin' hell" the old man snuffled.

Brother Martin smiled thinly. "So. Do you recognise each other? No – well, I know it's been a long time, and Norman here has been around – and I do mean *around* – around the whole wide world, hey, Norman?"

Then of course I suddenly knew who he was, this apparently feeble old man. "Norman? Uncle Norman? And now you'll both *have* to come in. And this place is in chaos," as I led the way, "I'm trying to tidy it up and get rid of some stuff." (Even then I was struggling to control my plethora of books and paper!) "But I'll make us tea, so just sit down and relax, and I can shout from the kitchen – but Uncle Norman? – it's so long since I saw you –"

Well, it was a bizarre occasion. Brother Martin was clearly glad to "take my weight off my feet" and mainly sat in silence. My Uncle

Norman was silent, too, slumped on the sofa. While I shouted inanities with simulated cheerfulness from the kitchen.

When I had brought in a tray with teapot and mugs, apologised for the lack of cookies, and poured tea into three mugs, I sat down near my two visitors.

Silence. We looked at each other, until I cleared my throat and exclaimed "What a surprise, Uncle Norman!" And then, stupidly, in sheer embarrassment, to break the silence – "Where have you been all my life?"

A sudden guffaw from Uncle Norman. Then more silence.

"I'm sure you know that Mum died a few years ago?" I persisted. "And Aunt Iris became a Nun, you probably know that too, she's in South Africa –"

Brother Martin put down his mug, cleared his throat and interrupted peremptorily. "I must go. But Derrick, if I may call you that – I'll telephone you later, sometime this evening, we need to talk. But Norman here needs to rest, I guess he's quite exhausted – so many changes and chances in one day, hey, Norman? –"

"But–"

"He needs a place to stay, Derrick? Just for tonight at least, and – this is very important, I'll explain later." Brother Martin was getting up. "And lock the door – any point of access – front-door, kitchen-door – this is very important. Right? The Police will be coming to see you both, later. And as you no doubt know, there's Witness Protection, they'll tell you all about it. For Norman. But I must go – and *lock the door behind me*, right?"

It surprises me that I can recall all this so clearly – though maybe I've invented some of the conversation. And details.

After Brother Martin had left, and after checking that I had locked the front-door behind him, I sat down again opposite my Uncle – still puzzled about his sudden appearance, so many years after his sudden *dis*appearance.

If my Mother had said anything after he left, all those years ago, it would probably have been "Good riddance to bad rubbish", one of her expressions of contempt. (She never liked Uncle Norman, who had once, apparently, insulted and embarrassed her "in front of my best friend".)

And nothing had been said later, to my memory – either about Uncle Norman; or my other uncle, Eddie, only brother of my Mother.

My young life had simply run on without them. And I can't say that I felt any strong emotional response *now* to Uncle Norman's sudden appearance. But when I returned to the living-room I was ready to initiate an exploratory conversation with him – only to find him slumped sideways on the sofa where he'd been sitting. He was snoring quietly.

After quickly making up the bed in the guest-bedroom, I tapped my Uncle on a shoulder and, when he opened his eyes, said "Come on, let's get you into bed, Uncle, hold on to me", helped him up, and led him into the bedroom. Where he promptly sat on the bed, groaned, took off his shoes, and slumped sideways. I lifted his legs and tried to make him more comfortable. And very soon he was snoring again – loudly.

Then I returned to my interrupted sorting and dispatching of old notes and old letters in old files. But now with the frequent distraction of unease about my Uncle and his sudden, mysterious reappearance in my life.

Brother Martin called as promised, in the early evening. I told him that my Uncle was still sound asleep; and that I was puzzled, troubled, about the situation.

"Well, I'm sorry – I apologise for just arriving like that – I did try to call you earlier, but no answer, I guess you were out. Anyway, I guessed it was going to be a surprise to you – I have to say it was a surprise to *me* when I realised he was probably your relative. But there's more, Derrick, can I call you Derrick, do you mind? – We are of course concerned about the situation – the Police have their hands full at the moment, but assured us that they will be contacting you soon. Maybe you don't know – of course you've been preoccupied with other things, tidying and tearing-up up old notes etcetera, you said – something I should be doing too. So maybe you don't know that there have been some local murders by let's call them Mafia Mob types – that old Hamilton thing, we all know about what happened in the past, Rocco Perri etcetera – some citizens are even proud of all that. But now two shootings, and other murders at a farm nearby, which the Police think are connected with a feud between the main two Mafia families. I'm only telling you all this because seems that your Uncle is involved – deeply involved, maybe – a witness to murder. So it seems that his life may be in danger – there have been threats, he admitted that – which is why I said to make sure your doors are locked at all times etcetera. Look, I don't want to frighten you, Derrick. But *you* should be careful too."

What could I say? "Thank you, I'll be careful. If anything happens –?'

"Call the Police immediately. Or 911. As I say, the Police will know about the situation, of course. As you probably know, there's a Witness Protection Programme. Maybe they'll – And of course the Police have your name and telephone number. Can you have your Uncle as a guest meanwhile? Until we know what he wants to do – or *can* do? Or what the Police want him to do. I hope he won't be any trouble. If there *are* problems – well, please don't hesitate –"

"If there are any problems, I'll call you immediately, Brother Martin. And of course the Police. Thank you for all you have done for my Uncle."

I should say here (why should I 'say here'? But why not?) that of course COVID continues to rule the world, provide endless statistics, and feed endless controversy. Across most countries. 176,156,662 worldwide 'confirmed cases'; 3,815,486 'confirmed deaths'. In Ontario: about 540,000 cases, nearly 9,000 deaths. So it goes. (But *Slaughterhouse-Five* hardly seems an appropriate reference. I hope.)

Maybe the Vaccines, which are becoming increasingly controversial, even before many countries are anywhere near the vaccin-ation-rate of the rich, privileged North American and European countries – maybe they will hold COVID and its now-many Variants at bay. Maybe they will even hold Death at bay, eventually? We hope!

As the wealthier countries 'open up' again, and the privileged young get back to partying and readying themselves to attend uni-versity, while their parents are again able to watch sports, attend con-certs, congregate in pubs and gyms – Maybe – maybe – But I'm sure not betting on it.

"It never rains but it pours." Another of my Mother's favourite say-ings. Why did that come into my fraying mind?

Back to my Uncle Norman. He slept through the night (though I did hear him once, perhaps twice, using the loo – Mum's very polite English expression).

And in the morning, he was waiting for me in the kitchen when I got up, rather late. I made some instant-coffee, and toasted two slices of rather elderly sliced-bread for him, as he sat slouched untidily at the kitchen-table.

"I'll have to go out and do a quick shop" I told him. "Cupboard's almost bare."

"Umph" he replied.

But he seemed satisfied with the toast and coffee.

"Did you sleep all right?" I asked him.

He belched; then "Yeah, not too bad. Now what?"

Which was my question too.

Suddenly he said, with what I took to be a dry laugh, "I remember you when you were just a baby. Now you're grown-up."

"Yes, but not much more mature, hey? That's what my wife – ex-wife – thought."

"Oh." Not even a smile. "Now what?"

"Well, I guess we can tell each other about our lives so far. You first!"

"Bloody stupid idea, Nephew." But he grinned, sarcastically. "I can tell you *my* life in one word – two words. After that War to end all wars. Fuckin' bloody mess. Three words. Drugs, more drugs. Jail, more jail. *Six* words. Don't have a fuckin' clue about how I can survive Outside. I'm too old and I don't bloody *care* now. Last time I was Out – Didn't that Father Marvin, whatever his name is, didn't he tell you anything about me?"

"Brother Martin. No, nothing personal, just that we must both be very careful and watchful – you can tell me why."

"*Why?* They bloody got spies everywhere, this is a fuckin' Mafia town, *you know that, you grew up here.* And word is that the bosses in the U.S. are pushing out our lot and I guess this town here is full of their guys ready to kill – *already* killed three here in two days, hey, and the local cops don't have a clue – well of course they don't, never did have – but what – And they know, the fuckin' Mafia, they know that I know – *what* I know – what I seen – " He stopped abruptly.

I sat in silence, waiting for him to continue. But after a few minutes, while he struggled to eat some toast with his, clearly, painfully worn-down teeth, he sighed heavily. "So, Nephew, you could say my time has come. And gone. The world doesn't fuckin' care. In fact, the world is just bloody glad to see the end of me, is what I think. And you know – *I'll be* glad to see the end of me."

"Don't say that, Uncle. We've only just – well, there are lots of things I want to ask you."

"Oh? But I got no answers for you, My Boy. My *Nephew*. We all got to make our way through this fuckin' world, *alone* – always on our bloody alone, whatever guys like our holy bloody Brother Whatsisname may say, whatever all those stuck-up Christian do-gooders may say who get a kick from prison-visiting, the ones who say they sad but they really enjoy enjoy seeing us guys shut away in prisons 'paying for our crimes against humanity' until we die, but none of them, *none of them*, has a fuckin' *clue* – So *well now* –"

But I could tell he was too tired to continue – too tired to answer any of my questions, participate in any conversation. So "Why don't you have a rest and then later we can talk?" I said.

* * * * *

And later, a couple hours later, we did converse further – after eating sandwiches that I made from the ancient bread, and drinking more of the lethal coffee. Uncle Norman was sitting on the sofa.

"Dad – my Father – what do you remember of him?"

"Fuckin' bloody Shit – Sorry. But you say you want the truth. So here it is. We hated him, Eddie and me, he was a bully and a liar. You really want to know? And in the War – well, he didn't go, of course, stayed back here and made money out of manufacting bombs and bullets – fuckin' coward. That factory he set up here in Hamilton, maybe it still exists, hey, I forgot to look – yes it sure bloody does, and the Mafia have been all over it, you bet they have! Still *are* all over it, and *in* it, I told the stupid Police that. So he gets rich – how *you* could go to university, hey? But he wouldn't help the rest of his family, no, no – especially the ones who had actually served this fuckin' country and saved it from Hitler and then the fuckin' Yellow Peril. But Eddie, he said to hell with all that and he – And even before that, he said to Hell with your fuckin' Father –"

"But, Uncle Norman, you must have known – Dad was born with a defective heart, something like those Blue Babies, I think – he nearly didn't survive at all – Mum always said that, *he* never did – and you must know he died quite young, he was only forty-three, I think. Didn't you know about that? Where were you then? When I asked Dad once, and then Mum after he died, just silence, silence -"

Uncle Norman coughed – he would have spat, outside, no doubt, but indoors he just swallowed the phlegm. And then he growled "Well, so where did *that* get us? Hey? What's the fuckin' point? The past is the past, we all gotta learn that. You can't change it. Never. But you said you would go and shop so we got something to eat, hey?"

"Yes. But just a few more questions, if you don't mind. What about Eddie – my Uncle Eddie – what happened to *him*?"

"We went to the War together. I told you that. He was always a good friend to me but – After the War, when we come back to Canada, and your Father wouldn't even give us jobs, he just – He went to the States, Eddie, I should of gone with him but I was always fuckin' stupid, he always called me Mister Slowpoke – but someone said he died in the Sixties – drugs, booze, who knows? And back here I got into the booze too, and drugs, and that was the start of *my* bad problems, with the Mafia here and the gangs – so I moved to Vancouver, more drugs, more booze – but things got bad there, real bad, so I come back here – But then, not so long ago, it's all *real* serious, hey – with Opioids, OxyContin, you know, the works – and I get hooked myself, nearly died – I was in Vancouver, ambulance got me to the hospital just in time, that's what a nurse told me when I woke up – but I got help there and then I come back here, like I say, and now I'm clean, *real clean*, better believe it – if you offered me Opioids right now, right now, I'd say 'Fuck off', I would, I bloody would, better believe it. – And that's enough, eh. Story of my stupid fuckin' life. But hey, I did serve my country, and your fuckin' Father, he didn't –"

"And what about your Sister – Iris?"

"Oh, *her*. When we get back from the War, she's gone all religious, doesn't even want to know about us, me and Eddie, we were destructive, *evil, evil. She said.* Did I kill any Germans, she said, and I said 'You better believe it, baby, *as many as I could*'. And after that she would barely talk to me at all, hardly even *look* at me. And your Mum and Dad, they wouldn't – And Eddie, you asked about him – the two of them, your Mum and Dad, they also just ignored *him*, even though he was your Mother's brother – and didn't I tell you how your Dad treated both of us, me and Eddie – how he wouldn't even fuckin' give us jobs? – his own brother –"

His voluble flow suddenly stopped and he slumped back on the sofa. After a few minutes, his eyes closed. And he started snoring.

He looked uncomfortable, but seemed so deeply asleep that I decided not to disturb him, and left him there when I set off for the supermarket; checking before I left that all the doors were locked.

It was a hot humid afternoon, I remember – typical Hamilton summer weather.

* * * * *

About an hour later, in mid-afternoon, I returned; lightly laden with some basic provisions. On the way, I had considered the situation, and decided it was necessary for me to contact Brother Martin again and ask for clearer information and advice from him and the Order, about my future relationship with Uncle Norman, and the extent of my responsibility for him. And what were the Police doing?

As I turned the corner and headed for my house, I felt a sudden unease. Silence, silence.

Then I saw him. Flat on his back at the side of the street. Half on and half off the sidewalk.

I ran towards him, throwing aside my two loaded bags.

He was breathing stertorously, blood oozing down his face from a small hole in his forehead, and dripping down to the street from a ragged wound in his chest.

"Uncle Norman, Uncle Norman." But his eyes were closed.

I sat on the kerb, and lifted him up, as well as I could. And became aware of a gathering crowd on the sidewalk. A woman shouted to me "The Police are coming, I called them."

Of course I had not expected him to go out and onto the street, alone, while I was away shopping.

And why did he?

It seemed like a deliberate act, a final confrontation with the Mafia assassin or whoever had now slaughtered him. He must have known they were waiting for him.

I think he was just tired of living. Death must have seemed his only option. So he went.

"So he went. And there was silence … silence and safety. And then, far away…"

One of my favourite poems when I first came across Great War Poetry, all those years ago, long before I met Pip. Siegfried Sassoon. The bravest of the brave: War Hero. And later the quintessential Pacifist: a true Peace-lover.

Just a few of those Great War poems at first, in my high-school

History class. And later, as a History Teacher, I tried to be careful in exposing my students to the most disturbingly intense of those poems. And even, when I could, I avoided reading some of them myself.

But it was, finally, Pip's intense engagement with those poems – his obvious love for them, and admiration for their creators – while he still remained very critical in his responsiveness; it was *his* engagement that called me into a final appreciation of what those poets had achieved. Facing death in the trenches or in No Man's Land, death by bomb or bullet or poison-gas or bayonet – or even by being blown up by a mine. Facing death, those poets yet retained their humanity to the very end. That's what we both saw.

And after long fervent argument, and close critical discussion, during the few weeks, the few days and nights, left in Pip's life, I knew *who* of all the poets represented in the Penguin text, and *which* of all the poems reprinted there, are for me the *ultimate glory, the paragon*.

"Well, all right," Pip said, "you have chosen, and of course I respect and fully accept your choice, though it isn't mine! So read it to me" and I did. Weeping as I ended. For what had gone, what was going, and what was still to go. What *is* still to go.

Isaac Rosenberg, "Dead Man's Dump". A poem that faces, encompasses, ultimate pain and sorrow, ultimate life and death; and spins unforgettable power from that human actuality; balancing, always, on the very edge of silence and existence.

A man's brains splattered on
A stretcher-bearer's face;
His shook shoulders slipped their load.
But when they bent to look again,
The drowning soul was sunk too deep
For human tenderness.

They left their dead with the older dead,
Stretched at the cross roads.

Burnt black by strange decay
Their sinister faces lie,
The lid over each eye.
The grass and coloured clay
More motion have than they,
Joined to the great sunk silences...

"Yes", Pip said. "A very great poem. The ultimate authority of Death. Its power, its majesty. But your original poem, by Siegfried Sassoon – the poem that, you told me, remember, first opened a door for you into Great War Poetry when you were a boy – I'll pick that one to die with. Because you were right then, as a boy. And now *I* can be right too, as a man. Your choice is now also mine. We are united, we are one."

Light many lamps and gather round his bed.
Lend him your eyes, warm blood, and will to live.
Speak to him, rouse him; you may save him yet.
He's young; he hated War; how should he die
When cruel old campaigners win safe through?

But death replied: 'I choose him.' So he went,
And there was silence in the summer night;
Silence and safety; and the veils of sleep.
Then, far away, the thudding of the guns.

Always, always, the thudding of the guns. Alas. But also silence, and safety. And death. And death. And death. And death.

And life? What of Life? Maybe we don't value it enough. Until we feel it ebbing away – *experience* it ebbing away. Until we know that 'our end is nigh'. Or until we observe it being stolen from others, and especially from children. (As is happening *now, right now,* in Ukraine – children, mothers, grandparents, slaughtered by Putin's Russian Army, in apartments, houses, basements – shopping, chatting with neighbours, walking to school –)

But what *is* it? One's life? A temporary existence on a dying planet circled by uncountable, *unimaginable* multitudes of distant universes – a very uncertain temporary individual existence, with some pleasures and much pain, in the midst of multitudes of creatures killing and consuming each other – all of them, all of us, living to die? Why? *Why?*

Yet – I still hope, with Oliver Sacks, that I will die feeling *Gratitude.* "I have loved and been loved, I have been given much and I have given something in return; I have read and travelled and thought and written… Above all, I have been a sentient being, a thinking animal, on this beautiful planet, and that in itself has been an enormous privilege and adventure." *Yes.*

But *please,* may those who follow us commit themselves to trying, *really trying,* to save this world, with all its present and future inhabitants, from the now-impending horrors of global warming. Illogical? Yes. But – *Please.*

Words like salt-cold salt-smooth salt-burning stones:
sounds like the sounds of the waves of the sea.

"Oh build your ship of death, for you will need it"
"bones are scattered at the grave's mouth"
"If I should die, think only this of me"
"Just a little white with the dust"
"Time held me green and"
"I am sick, I must die"
"Ripeness is all"
"The years"
"You"
"I"

We are and are not.